Ao Bc [illegible]

Con

The Crow and the Jug

Long ago, in a jungle, there once lived a crow. One day, he was very thirsty and he went in search of water. It was a very hot day and his thirst increased. But there was no water to be seen anywhere!

The crow reached a village, and thought, "Oh! Hopefully I will find water here."

He flew to the village well and was about to drink his fill when some naughty boys chased him away. He flew to the top of a hut and looked around. He spotted a jug of water kept near the door of a house.

The crow flew down towards the jug and put his beak in to drink water from it. But sadly, there was very little water in it and his beak could not reach it.

Just then, a young boy threw a stone at the crow. It missed him and landed in the jug. The water level rose a bit. The crow saw this and was delighted. He picked up the pebbles lying nearby and put them inside the jug one by one till the water level rose.

The crow drank the water from the jug happily. Satisfied, he flapped his wings and flew away, cawing loudly.

When you are in trouble, don't give up.

The Lapwings and the Sea

A lapwing couple lived by a beautiful seashore. The wife, who was about to lay the eggs, said to her husband, "Dear, I don't want to lay the eggs by the seashore. The evil sea might take our eggs away. The eggs will be safe by a pond or a lake."

The husband understood his wife's concern. But he said, "Dear, don't worry! If the sea takes our eggs, I will surely teach him a lesson."

The wife then laid the eggs in their nest. But alas! When the lapwings went looking for food, the sea rose up and swallowed their eggs.

The angry husband called a meeting of all the birds and said, "Dear friends! The sea has eaten my eggs today. Tomorrow he will eat your eggs. Let's tell the king about this injustice." They went to the eagle, who was their king.

The eagle was very upset on hearing what had happened and promised the birds that he would punish the sea by sucking it dry.

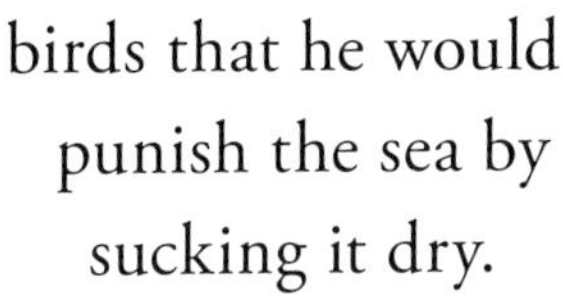

Lord Vishnu overheard them. He felt sorry for the birds and decided to help them. He threatened the sea, asking it to return the lapwing's eggs.

The Sea God realised his mistake and returned the lapwings' eggs.

Stand up against injustice and cruelty.

The Donkey and the Cunning Fox

Once, the lion, the king of the jungle, was severely wounded while fighting with an elephant. Hungry and powerless, he said to his senior minister, the fox, “I cannot hunt. Find me a prey to eat.”

The fox went deep into the forest to look for a prey. There he met a donkey. The cunning fox said to the donkey, “The king is looking for a bodyguard. I am sure you will fit the job.”

The donkey was happy and followed the fox. As soon as the lion saw the donkey, he pounced on him. But he missed and the donkey ran away.

The fox ran after the donkey and told him, “The king was only testing your alertness and is very pleased with you. Let’s go back.”

This time, the lion hid behind a bush. As soon as the donkey arrived, he pounced on him and killed him.

Before the lion could eat the donkey, the fox asked him to take a bath and say his prayers. When the lion went away, the fox ate the donkey’s brain.

When the lion returned and asked about the missing brain, the fox replied, "Your majesty, a donkey has no brain!"

Being smart is better than being intelligent.

The Snake Gets Married

In a village, a childless couple prayed to God every day for a baby.

One day, their wish was granted. The wife became pregnant and gave birth to a baby nine months later. But, to their shock, the baby was not human; it was a snake! Still, the couple brought up the snake like their son.

When the snake was old enough to get married, they started becoming worried. Who would marry a snake? The man told his friend about his problem.

His friend assured him, "Dear friend, my daughter will marry your son."

The snake and the girl got married and the new bride looked after her snake-husband dutifully.

One night, the man noticed that his snake-son crawled out of his basket and turned into a man. Then, after a while, he went back into his snakeskin.

The next night, when the snake came out of his skin, the man threw the snakeskin into the fire. The son thanked his father and said, "Father, due to a curse, I had to become a snake. But I was promised that when someone, without asking me, destroyed the snakeskin, I would become a man again. By burning the skin, you have broken the curse. I will never turn into a snake now."

The couple lived happily with their son and his wife.

Every bad situation has something good about it.

Death and Lord Indra's Parrot

One day, all the Gods held a meeting at Lord Indra's heavenly abode. Lord Indra had a pet parrot which he loved very much. The parrot always sat on Lord Indra's arm.

The Lord of Death was the last one to enter the court. When the Lord entered, he looked at the parrot and smiled. The parrot understood that he would die soon.

All the Gods knew that Lord Indra loved the parrot a lot. So, they all pleaded with the Lord of Death to spare the parrot's life. However, the Lord told them that death was decided by Destiny and he could not do anything about it.

All the Gods requested Destiny to spare the parrot's life. Destiny replied that it was Death who took these decisions.

So, all the Gods once again pleaded with Death to spare the parrot's life. But, as soon as Death looked at the parrot, it died. Everybody in the court was very sad.

Death consoled the Gods by saying, “Every living being has to die one day – be it a beggar or a king. Death is common to all and everyone dies one day.”

All that lives must die one day.

The Loyal Mongoose

In a village, a poor couple lived with their baby boy, whom they loved deeply. They also had a pet mongoose, a playmate for the baby.

One day, the mother went to fetch water, leaving the child with the father. Some people from the village called him away to perform a

puja immediately. He left his baby in the care of the mongoose, since the baby was sleepy.

The dutiful mongoose sat by the cradle in which the baby slept peacefully. Shortly, the mongoose noticed a black snake slithering into the room. He pounced on the snake, and after a fight, killed him.

With his mouth and paws covered with the snake's blood, the mongoose sat by the main door, awaiting the return of the parents. The mother, seeing the mongoose covered in blood, thought that he had killed her baby. Angry, she threw the water-pitcher on the mongoose, killing him on the spot. She ran inside to her baby.

She saw a dead snake on the floor and her baby sleeping peacefully in the cradle. She guessed what had happened and realised her mistake. But, it was too late. Her pet mongoose was dead.

Do not be hasty.

The Four Friends and the Hunter

A deer, a mouse and a crow were very good friends.

One day, a turtle visited them, and asked, "Can I also be your friend?"

The three friends were very kind and allowed the turtle to join their group. A few days later, a hunter came to the jungle. Seeing him, the crow flew away, the mouse ran into a hole and the deer hid behind the bushes. However, the poor turtle moved so slowly that the hunter caught him before he could hide.

The three friends made a plan to save him. The crow flew high up and spotted the hunter walking by the river. As planned, the deer pretended to be dead, and lay down in the hunter's path. The excited hunter, seeing the deer, left the turtle on the ground and ran towards the deer. Meanwhile, the mouse nibbled on the net and freed the turtle. When the hunter neared the deer, the deer sprang up and ran away.

The hunter returned to where he had left the turtle, but he, too, had crawled away. The hunter left the jungle and never came back. Thereafter, the four friends lived happily together.

A friend in need is a friend indeed.

The Thoughtless Crow

Once upon a time, there was a large gathering of birds. There were swans, parrots, ducks, cuckoos, peacocks, pigeons, doves and many others. They had assembled to discuss a matter of great concern. They were discussing that though Garud was the king of the birds, he did not take care of them well.

Therefore, the birds decided to elect a new king. After much discussion, they decided to make the owl their king.

While the birds were preparing to coronate their new king, a crow joined in and mocked, "How shameful it will be to have an owl as our king. He is so ugly and cannot even see during the day. Besides, he feeds on the other birds. How will he protect us?"

The birds agreed with the crow.

The owl, who was waiting to be coronated, did not know what was causing the delay. He asked his assistant, "Why is it so quiet? When will the birds coronate me?"

The assistant told the owl what the crow had said.

The wise owl saw the crow and said, "Because of you I will not be made the king! From now on, you are my greatest enemy."

The crow felt sorry but it was too late to seek forgiveness.

Think before you speak.

The Swan's Visit

A beautiful swan lived alone by a pond. One day, an owl made a nearby tree its home too. With time, they became good friends.

During summer, when the pond became dry, the owl decided to return to its previous home. He invited the swan to join him. However, the swan said that she would live by a small river, half a mile away from the pond. But, she promised to visit the owl whenever she missed him.

After a few months, the swan started missing the owl. So, she flew to where the owl lived. The owl was glad to meet his friend again. They had dinner together and the tired Swan went to bed early. The owl perched himself on the tree bark.

At night, some travellers took shelter under the tree. When he saw them, the owl hooted loudly. The travellers thought that it was a bad omen and shot an arrow at the owl.

Since, the owl could see at night, he flew away. But the arrow hit the sleeping swan instead and killed her.

Choose your friends carefully.

A Poor Man's Dream

Once, a poor man lived in a village, begging for alms every day. Whatever food he received as alms, he stored in an earthen pot.

One afternoon, the poor man was lying on his cot and dreaming of getting beautiful

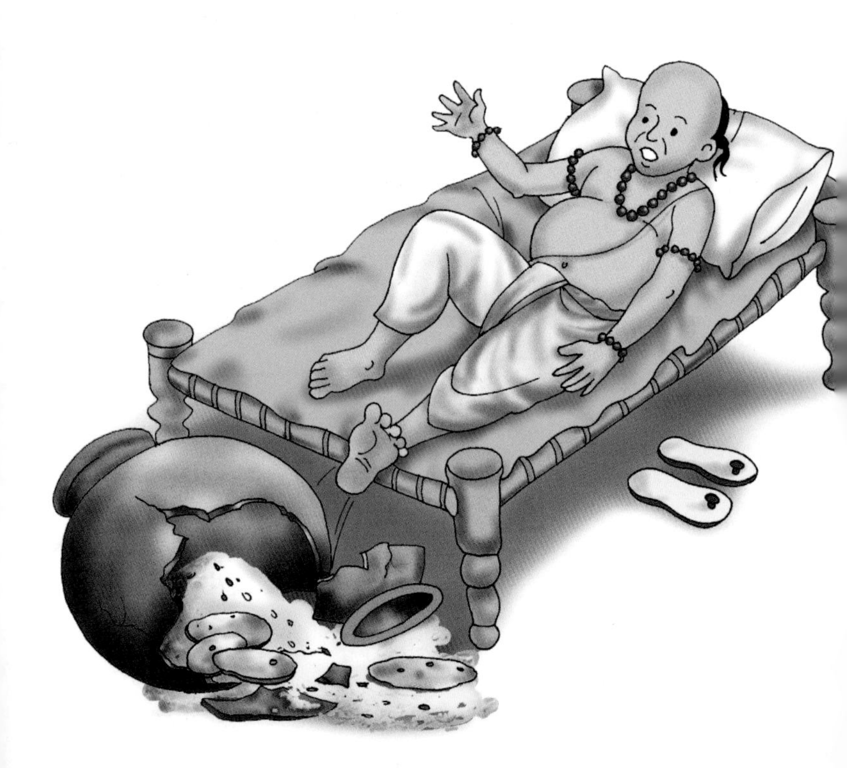

things. He imagined himself wearing expensive clothes and eating good food.

Then, he imagined that he was the owner of a big shop and had many customers. He earned lots of money and bought a cow and a buffalo. The cow and the buffalo gave birth to young ones. When these young ones grew up, he started to sell milk and curd in the market. He became richer and bought a big house for himself.

While the man was imagining these fancy things, he began to move his legs rapidly in the air in excitement. By mistake, his legs hit the earthen pot. The pot fell down and broke to pieces.

The man got up with a start and saw that he was still poor and was lying in his hut. He also saw that he had kicked his earthen pot and all the food stored in it had scattered on the floor.

Hard work is better than daydreaming.

The Peacock and the Fox

A fox saw a beautiful peacock sitting on the topmost branch of a tree in the forest where he lived. He thought, "I wish I could eat

this peacock! But I cannot climb up the tree. It is too high for me!"

He thought of a plan and asked the peacock, "Why are you sitting on the tree? Don't you know that all the animals of this forest have decided not to kill each other for food?"

"Oh, you mean that the lion, tiger and leopard will eat grass from today?" asked the peacock.

The clever fox replied, "Come down and let's ask the king about this."

"Sure, but I can see your friends, the hounds, coming towards this tree. We can ask them," said the peacock.

"Hounds! I have to go!" the fox exclaimed. The hounds were his enemy.

"But, why do you run away? You just said that all the animals and birds have become friends," said the peacock.

"The hounds might not have heard of this decision yet," said the fox and ran away as fast as he could.

Think before you leap.

Somilaka, the Weaver

A weaver called Somilaka was very sad because he felt that the other weavers were richer than he. He decided to end his life. He wove himself a rope of grass and hung the noose around his neck.

Just as he was about to hang himself, he heard a voice, "Wait! It is me - God! I am happy with your hard work. Ask for any wish and it shall be granted."

Somilaka said, "I am poor and unhappy. Please make me wealthy."

God agreed, but said, "First, you must meet two families; one that has 'Secret Wealth' but does not spend any of it and the other that has 'Useful Wealth' and makes good use of it."

Somilaka first visited the family with the 'Secret Wealth'. There, he was greeted by a very rich but rude man. The family members fought with each other and were misers.

Next, he went to the family with the 'Useful Wealth'. There, he was greeted with smiles, served delicious food and taken care of.

Somilaka thought, "The family with the

'Useful Wealth' does not have much money but is happy and kind."

He said to God, "Please make me happy as happiness is much more important than riches."

Happiness is the biggest wealth of all.

A Dog Goes Abroad

Once upon a time, there lived a dog called Chitranga.

Now, sadly, it had not rained for many days in Chitranga's country. All the animals were hungry and thirsty. Chitranga

thought, “I should move to a country where I can find food and water!”

Chitranga left his home and reached a new country. He entered a house through an open window and found lots of delicious food inside. Luckily, there was no one in the house, so, he happily ate his fill. As he was leaving the house, the dogs of the new country began to chase and bite him.

The next day, he was hungry again. He decided to try his luck at the same house. He found more food but was bitten by the same dogs when leaving.

Chitranga was scared. He cried, “I cannot go on like this. I must return to my own country and live in peace than be bitten every day.”

Soon, he returned home. Upon his return, Chitranga’s relatives and friends came to meet him. They asked him about the new country.

He said, “There is plenty to eat in the new land, but sadly, no friends to keep you happy.”

East or West, home is the best.

The Tree and the Weaver

Once, there lived a weaver called Mantharaka. One day, while weaving, his wooden loom broke down. He thought, "I need wood to make a new loom."

So, he went to a forest and was about to cut

a tree. Just then, a voice called out, "Stop! Please don't cut this tree! It is my home!"

Mantharaka was surprised to hear the voice. He said, "I need this wood to make a new loom." He raised his axe again.

"I shall grant you any wish if you leave this tree alone," begged the voice.

Mantharaka said, "I must ask my wife and friends." On his way home, Mantharaka met his friend, the barber.

"You must wish that you become a king," advised the barber.

"Let me ask my wife, too," thought Mantharaka.

His wife said, "As a king, you'll have to fight hard battles. Ask for an extra pair of hands and a head. You can earn more money by weaving extra yarn."

Mantharaka hurried back to the forest and asked for his wish. Soon, he had two pairs of hands and one extra head. The villagers thought that he was a monster and chased him out of the village.

Do not follow advice blindly.

The Jackal and the Drum

One day, when wandering in the jungle looking for food, a hungry jackal named Gomaya reached a battlefield. A young tree stood in the corner of the battlefield. Under the tree was a battle-drum.

When the wind blew, a low-lying branch of the tree

touched the side of the drum and produced a soft drumbeat.

Hearing the drumbeat, Gomaya thought, foolishly, “I am sure that there is an animal trapped inside the drum! If I can get him out, I will eat him up.”

Unfortunately, Gomaya could not tear the thick fabric of the drum.

Hearing the drumbeat, a leopard came there. Gomaya said to the leopard, “Your majesty! An animal is hiding inside the drum. You can use your strong teeth and sharp claws to tear the drum.”

When the leopard tore open the drum and found it empty, he said to Gomaya in anger, “You foolish liar! The drum is empty. I will eat you instead, now!”

Saying this, the leopard pounced on Gomaya and ate him.

Do not be greedy and foolish.

Titles in ILLUSTRATED 15 STORIES

001–048

Aesop's Fables
SET OF 48 BOOKS

049–060

Akbar and Birbal
SET OF 12 BOOKS

061–080

Bible Stories
SET OF 20 BOOKS

081–088

Tenali Raman
SET OF 8 BOOKS

089–094

Panchatantra Stories
SET OF 6 BOOKS

095–114

Arabian Nights
SET OF 20 BOOKS